This igloo book belongs to:

....

igloobooks

Published in 2018
by Igloo Books Ltd
Cottage Farm
Sywell
NN6 0BJ
www.igloobooks.com

REX001 0418
2 4 6 8 10 9 7 5 3 1
ISBN 978-1-78810-909-3

Written by Sienna Williams
Illustrated by Jo Byatt

Designed by Alex Alexandrou
Edited by Stephanie Moss

Printed and manufactured in China

Sienna Williams

Jo Byatt

Dragon
to the Rescue

igloobooks

Albert was new at school and he felt quite nervous and shy.
He watched the other dragons **loop-the-loop** around the sky.

Whoosh!

went the scorching flames...

... as fire **swirled** around the air.

Albert was so amazed that he stopped to look and stare.

When Albert asked to have a go, he learned the teacher's special rule.

"To make sure that you're safe, you must only breathe fire at school!"

Albert understood, but his classmates whispered together...

... "Those school rules are silly. We should forget them forever!"

In next day's fire class, everyone performed like a pro.

Albert started to feel nervous and then it was his go.

Albert **spluttered...**

... and **coughed.**

Then he let out a...

... **loud croak!**

But instead of flames of fire, he coughed up little puffs of smoke!

Albert felt confused. He took one more deep breath and blew.

He closed his eyes, but this time, he **sneezed** a smoky...

"**He can't do it,**" said the dragons.

"**He shouldn't be here!**" they cried.

So, poor Albert flew away from school, to find somewhere to hide.

Albert came across a waterfall where he could sit and think.

His throat felt so dry from coughing that he had a long, cool drink.

He took **gulp** after **gulp**, until his cheeks bulged large and round.

But suddenly, Albert paused when he heard a familiar sound.

There were flames going **whoosh** as the naughty dragons flew about.

Albert was so surprised, he couldn't help **spitting** his water out!

His classmates couldn't believe it. They watched their flames all disappear.

"What are you doing?" cried Albert. **"You know you can't breathe fire here!"**

Albert felt so **angry.** He shouted **louder** than ever before. Suddenly, before he knew it, he let out a great big, **fiery...**

ROAR

"I can breathe fire after all!" cried Albert. "My throat is cured," he said.

"But I like being different. I want to be a firefighter instead!"

RR!

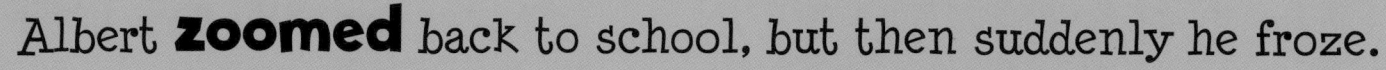

Albert **zoomed** back to school, but then suddenly he froze.

Before he arrived, a smoky smell went up his nose!

"We kept on breathing fire," one of the naughty dragons cried.

"But we couldn't put it out, no matter how hard we all tried."

"I know how to help," said Albert. **"Don't worry, everyone."**

He took a gulp of water...

... then with a **hiss,** the flames were gone.

"Thank you!" they all cried. "You're the bravest dragon in the land!
We always thought the rules were silly, but now we understand."

The next day at school, Albert arrived to **claps** and **cheers.**
Now he'd found his talent, he forgot all of his fears.

Well Done, Albert!

Suddenly he was a hero and his teacher thought so, too.

Now when he grew up, Albert knew just what he would do.